Adventures Abound

Exciting Short Stories for Kids

Sayan Panda

Ukiyoto Publishing

All global publishing rights are held by

Ukiyoto Publishing

Published in 2024

Content Copyright © Sayan Panda

ISBN 9789362692146

All rights reserved.
No part of this publication may be reproduced,
transmitted, or stored in a retrieval system, in any
form by any means, electronic, mechanical,
photocopying, recording or otherwise, without the
prior permission of the publisher.

The moral rights of the author have been asserted.

This is a work of fiction. Names, characters, businesses, places, events, locales, and incidents are either the products of the author's imagination or used in a fictitious manner. Any resemblance to actual persons, living or dead, or actual events is purely coincidental.

This book is sold subject to the condition that it shall
not by way of trade or otherwise, be lent, resold, hired
out or otherwise circulated, without the publisher's
prior consent, in any form of binding or cover other
than that in which it is published.

www.ukiyoto.com

To my little angel Arya

Contents

The Magic Telescope	1
Aarya and the Magic Compass	3
Twinkle the Little Start	5
The Dancing Shadows	7
Physics of Flight	9
Explorer	11
The Jungle Homes	13
The Seed and Scruffy	16
The Telepathic Village	18
Aaryan and Robo	21
The Mysterious Disappearance	23
The Curious Student	25
The Sleepy Moon	27
The Mischievous Wind	30
The Shining Stars	33
Life on Mars	36
The First Snow	38
The Magical Garden	40
The Butterfly Kingdom	43
The Lonely Chameleon	47
Raju The Wizard	50
The Great Migration	53

Fluffy's Big Night	56
What is Happiness?	58
The Case of the Missing Mushrooms	61
The Magical Bedroom	65
Open Mind	68
The First Snow	71
No More Afraid	74
Tiny Droplet	77
About the Author	*80*

The Magic Telescope

Shruti was a very curious 8-year-old girl who loved gazing up at the night sky. She would spend hours trying to spot different planets, stars and constellations. One day, as she was stargazing from her bedroom window, she noticed something strange. A small package had appeared on her desk.

Shruti opened the package and found a note that said "For your curiosity - use it well!" Inside was a golden telescope unlike any she had seen before. It was small enough to hold in her hands but had strange runes and symbols carved all over it. When she peered through the eyepiece, she gasped. She could see planets and stars so close; it was as if she could touch them!

"This must be a magic telescope!" she thought excitedly. She decided to use it to explore the solar system and satisfy her endless curiosity. First, she focused the telescope on Mercury and was amazed to see volcanoes spewing lava on its surface. Next, she viewed Venus and its dense atmosphere wrapped all around the planet.

On Mars, she spotted dust storms raging across its rusty red landscape. She noticed two small moons, Phobos and Deimos, orbiting the planet. Past Mars was the asteroid belt, filled with countless rocky chunks of material left over from the formation of the planets.

Shruti spotted the dwarf planet Ceres among the asteroids.

When she looked at Jupiter, the largest planet, its Great Red Spot jumped out at her. She saw three of Jupiter's 79 moons - Io, Europa and Ganymede. Saturn surprised her with its magnificent rings, made of countless pieces of icy material. Its moons, Titan and Enceladus, looked colourful under the magic telescope.

Uranus showed Shruti its unique sideways tilt as it orbited the sun. Its five largest moons - Miranda, Ariel, Umbriel, Titania and Oberon - floated around the aquamarine planet. Neptune was the farthest known planet from the sun as she observed its swirling blue-green atmosphere and winds gusting at 1500 miles per hour. Its largest moon Triton had geysers gushing icy particles.

After her wondrous tour of the solar system with her magic telescope, Shruti had learned so much. Her curiosity about space had been satisfied but had also been sparked even more. She couldn't wait to see what more mysteries the universe held!

Aarya and the Magic Compass

Aarya was an 8 year old boy who loved exploring the forest near his home in the mountains. One day, as he was venturing deep into the woods, he suddenly lost track of which way was home. He turned around and around trying to figure out the path but everywhere looked the same.

"I'm lost!" cried Aarya worriedly. That's when he heard a tiny voice say "Over here!". Aarya turned around and saw his old compass lying on the ground. Except this compass was talking!

"Who said that?" asked a surprised Aarya. "I did!" replied the compass. "My name is Compass and I'm a magic compass. I can help you find your way home."

"Wow a talking compass! Can you really help me?" asked Aarya excitedly. "Of course, that's what I'm here for. Do you know which direction is which?" asked Compass.

Aarya shook his head no. "Then let me teach you. I always point towards North. So when the arrow is pointing that way, you will be going North," said Compass.

Aarya turned Compass around slowly understanding where each direction was. "Got it! So that way is North.

Then the opposite side must be South." said Aarya confidently.

"Correct!" said Compass. " The direction to your right is East and direction to your left is West. Now you know the four main directions. I will help guide you home safely."

With Compass to guide him, Aarya was able to learn his way around the forest. Whenever he came to a fork in the path, Compass would point him North, South, East or West depending on which way was right.

Soon the forest started looking familiar. After a while, Aarya spotted his favorite big tree in the distance. He had reached the edge of the forest near his village.

"We made it! Thank you Compass for teaching me about directions and helping me find my way back home," said a relieved Aarya.

"You're very welcome. Remember to always check your compass if you ever feel lost. And don't wander too deep into the forest without me," said Compass.

From that day on, Aarya and his magic compass Compass went on many wonderful adventures in the forest. And Aarya always made sure to pay attention to which direction was which so he never got lost again.

Twinkle the Little Start

Twinkle was a little star who lived up in the night sky. She shone brightly each evening along with all the other stars. But Twinkle had a secret - she was afraid of the dark.

While all the other stars would shine proudly throughout the night, Twinkle would start to dim her light as soon as the sun went down. She didn't like how big and dark the sky became without the sun. All she could see were the other bright stars, but there were still shadows everywhere in between.

"What if something is hiding in the dark?" Twinkle thought to herself. "Something that could blow me out or make me fall from the sky!" So each night she would shine a little bit less until she was barely glowing at all.

The other stars noticed that Twinkle wasn't shining as bright. "Why are you dimming your light Twinkle?" they asked her. But Twinkle was too embarrassed to admit she was scared of the dark. She would just say she was tired.

One night, a big full moon was out. It shone so brightly it almost looked like daytime. "Maybe tonight I won't be so scared" thought Twinkle. But as soon as the last bit of sun went down, her light started to fade like always.

Suddenly, Twinkle saw three shooting stars zip across the sky. "Wow, what are those?" she wondered. She followed their path and saw they were landing down on the earth below. Twinkle was curious but also scared - she had never left the safety of the night sky before.

She took a deep breath and slowly started to shoot down towards the earth. The closer she got, the more she could see thanks to the moonlight - there were fields and trees and a big lake down below. And she saw the three shooting stars she had been following.

As she got very close to touching down on the ground, Twinkle saw that the shooting stars were actually three little fireflies! Their tails lit up and glowed different colors. "Hi there!" they called up to Twinkle, "Why are you visiting us down here?"

Twinkle told them all about how she was afraid of the dark. The fireflies explained that down on the ground it doesn't seem so dark at all with the moon and stars providing enough light. And they were never afraid because they had each other to light up the night together.

Twinkle realized she didn't need to be afraid either as long as she kept shining bright. From that night on, Twinkle glowed with the most brilliant light of all the stars. And she wasn't scared of the dark sky anymore because she knew down below, the moon, stars and fireflies were there keeping the nighttime from ever being too scary or too lonely.

The Dancing Shadows

Rehaan smiled as the afternoon sunlight filtered through the trees, creating dancing shadows all around the backyard. It had been a long day at school and he was enjoying some free time before dinner.

As Rehaan lay in the grass, watching the shadows shift and change shapes, his imagination began to run wild. One shadow in particular caught his eye - it looked like a long-armed monkey swinging from branch to branch. "Hello Mr. Monkey," he said with a giggle. "Where are you going in such a hurry?"

To his surprise, the shadow monkey stopped and turned to him. "I'm looking for bananas to eat!" it replied in a high-pitched voice. "Do you know where I can find some?" Rehaan laughed and pointed to a nearby tree. "I think I saw some up there. But be careful - there's also a lion sleeping under that tree!"

The shadow monkey's eyes grew wide with fear and it quickly scurried up the tree trunk. Rehaan watched with delight as it started munching on bananas, keeping an eye out for the sleeping lion below. But soon, another shape emerged from the shadows - it was the figure of a tall giraffe, its neck stretching up towards the clouds.

"Good afternoon!" the giraffe said to the monkey. "Do you mind if I grab a banana or two? I'm feeling a bit peckish." The monkey nodded and pointed the giraffe towards the best bananas. But just then, a rustling came from the grass below. The lion was waking up!

Rehaan's heart started pounding - what would happen between the animals? Would the lion chase after the monkey and giraffe for invading its naptime? He watched eagerly as the lion slowly rose to its feet, yellow eyes blinking sleepily in the sunlight. It let out a huge yawn...and then smiled up at the tree.

"Don't worry friends, you're welcome to the bananas," the lion said kindly. "I'm not hungry right now anyway. In fact, would you like to join me for naptime in the shade?" Rehaan's eyes widened - what an unexpected turn of events! The monkey and giraffe looked at each other and shrugged. Then they all settled down together for a peaceful rest.

With the animals no longer providing any entertainment, Rehaan's gaze moved to a new shadow taking shape. He smiled, ready for his imagination to transport him to fantastical new lands filled with adventures and friendship. The dancing shadows were surely just getting started!

Physics of Flight

It was a bright summer afternoon and Shreshtha was playing in the garden when she noticed a bumblebee struggling to fly against the wind. "Poor little bee, the wind is too strong!" she thought.

The bumblebee seemed determined not to give up. After many failed attempts at taking off, it finally managed to get airborne but was blown sideways by the gusts of wind.

Shreshtha watched curiously as the plump little bee named Beebee kept correcting its course with small adjustments of its wings. "It must be very hard work to fly in such windy conditions," she said to herself.

Just then, Beebee landed nearby on a flower. "Why hello there!" said Beebee. "I couldn't help noticing you watching me fly around. Do you have any questions?"

"Yes!" replied Shreshtha. "How do you manage to fly when it's so windy? It looks so difficult."

Beebee buzzed with excitement, always happy to explain the science behind its flying abilities. "Well, did you know that bee wings are designed perfectly for flight?" it began.

It went on to describe how the structure and movement of its wings created lift, allowing it to overcome gravity and fly. Beebee also talked about using its senses and muscle control to continuously adjust its wing position for stable flight even in unpredictable winds.

By the end of the conversation, Shreshtha had learned so much. She realized that flying was truly an amazing feat that took a lot of skill, effort and ingenious adaptations.

"Thank you for explaining it so well, Beebee!" said Shreshtha. "I have a new appreciation for how hard you little bees work to fly. You're very brave!"

Beebee buzzed happily. "You're most welcome. Now if you'll excuse me, this wind isn't going to blow itself! I'd better get back to work." With that, the determined little bumblebee took off once more into the breezy skies.

Explorer

Souvik lived in a small village in India. From a young age, he was fascinated by the world outside his village. He would spend hours poring over his geography books, reading all about different places with their varying landscapes, people, cultures and most interestingly - climates.

"I want to travel everywhere and learn about how weather can be so different in faraway lands!" Souvik told his mother. His mother smiled indulgently at her curious son. She knew his heart lay in exploration, not in settling down in the village like others.

On his 12th birthday, Souvik's parents surprised him with a gift - a backpack and a globe. "This is so you can start your exploration, even if it's through books for now" his father said. Souvik was overjoyed. He spent days spinning the globe, letting his fingers wander across oceans and continents, wondering what each place would be like.

He read all he could find about tropical rainforests and the heavy rainfall they received. He was amazed by the huge trees and diverse wildlife in those jungles. He read about hot deserts where it hardly ever rained but temperatures soared during the day. The arid landscape and desert animals fascinated him.

One day, Souvik decided to write letters to pen pals around the world, asking them about the climate and wildlife in their area. Weeks later, he received his first reply - from a boy named Jake living in Canada. Jake told him about their cold winters with snow falling thick and blankets of white covering the land. Souvik was thrilled by the descriptions of ice skating on frozen lakes and snowball fights. He bundled up in blankets just imagining the chill.

More letters came - from Maia in Brazil talking about the tropical heat and rainforests, Isaac in Kenya speaking of dry savannahs and grazing animals, Asha in Australia detailing the beaches and coral reefs. Souvik spent hours outside each day, pretending he was in these new places, feeling the sunshine or wrapping up against an imaginary cool breeze.

His dream was one day experiencing it all for real. And so, as Souvik grew, he studied hard, saving every rupee. After years of preparation, the day finally came when his parents sent him off on a world tour. Souvik explored jungles, deserts, tundras - feeling varied climates on his skin, meeting people with different ways of living. It was the adventure of a lifetime. Souvik had found his calling - to share his wonder of the world with others through his travels and stories.

The Jungle Homes

Aarya was always curious about the forest that surrounded his village. Though his parents had warned him not to venture in alone, his curiosity often got the better of him. One Saturday, when his parents were busy in the fields, he decided to explore the jungle.

Armed with his bag that had a bottle of water and some cookies, Aarya entered the dense forest. It was much cooler under the shade of the big trees. He walked slowly, looking all around, hoping to catch a glimpse of some animals.

After sometime, he heard a rustling sound above him. Looking up, he saw a monkey family sitting on a branch. "Hello! I am Aarya. Can you tell me about where you live?" he asked.

The older monkey came down and said, "We live high up in the trees to stay safe. My name is Raju. My family and I live in this Banyan tree. It has lots of branches that give us shelter. We also find plenty of fruits to eat like figs and berries. The trees protect us from predators on the ground like lions and tigers. It also keeps us cool in the hot afternoons. Come, I'll show you our home."

Raju climbed up quickly with Aarya holding onto his tail. They reached a cluster of branches with leaves woven together. Inside were two baby monkeys playing. "This is where my wife Rani and I live with our babies. We feel secure up high and can keep a lookout for danger while resting," explained Raju.

Aarya was fascinated. He thanked Raju for showing him their tree home and climbed down. He continued walking and soon reached a small stream. On the bank, he saw a deer drinking water. "Hello! Can you tell me about where you live?"

The deer looked up, "My name is Lali. My family lives near this stream in a grassy meadow. We like to live close to a source of water. The long grass provides good camouflage and food. When lions or tigers come near, we can run fast into the tall grass and they cannot spot us. After drinking water in the morning, we graze in the meadow throughout the day."

Aarya nodded listening closely. Just then, a rustle in the bushes made Lali run away swiftly. From the bushes emerged a leopard calling out to her cubs. "Hello little man. I'm Leela and these are my babies - Leeu and Leeloo. We live in a hidden cave in the dense trees where no other animal can find us. It gives us protection from larger predators while we hunt. That's why we chose to make our home near this stream, so water is also close by. Do you want to see our home?"

Aarya agreed, a little nervously. Leela led him carefully to a thicket of bushes. Pulling the leafy cover aside, she revealed a small cave. Inside were two baby leopards playing. "Our den keeps us safe from other threats.

What do you think of our jungle homes?" Leela asked with a gentle purr.

Aarya was amazed by all the different habitats. He thanked Leela and said goodbye to the leopard family. As he walked back happily, thinking of all that he had learned, he bumped into a big elephant! "Oops, sorry mister elephant! Can you please tell me about where you live?"

The elephant laughed, "No problem little one. My name is Gajraj. Elephants like me live in herds. We migrate around the forest in groups, searching for food and water. When it's time to rest, we look for an open grassy clearing near a watering hole or river. My family and I love to take mud baths and dust baths to stay cool and protected from insects. We also communicate with each other over long distances by making trumpeting sounds."

Aarya smiled, "Thank you for telling me about elephant homes Gajraj ji. I have learned so much today about all the different animal habitats. I should get back before it gets dark. Thanks to all the animal friends who told me about where they live."

Waving goodbye to Gajraj, he happily made his way out of the forest with a smile, looking forward to share his new discoveries with his parents. Aarya had a newfound love for the jungle and understood that even though each animal home was unique, they all lived together in harmony in the forest.

The Seed and Scruffy

Little Seed was starting his journey in the big world. He had just fallen from his mother tree and was now resting on the soft forest floor. "Wow, the world is so big out here!" thought Seed. He looked around at all the fallen leaves, bugs crawling by, and tall trees towering over him. It was a new exciting place but also a little scary.

"I wonder what I'm supposed to do now?" Seed asked himself. Just then, a curious squirrel named Scruffy was foraging for food nearby. He spotted Seed and scurried over. "Well, hello there little fella! Welcome to the forest. My name is Scruffy," he said with a smile. "I'm Seed," replied Seed nervously.

"The first thing you need to do Seed is find the perfect spot to grow. Somewhere with soil, sunshine and room to stretch your roots. I'll help you look," offered Scruffy. They searched all over until Scruffy spotted a nice patch of soft earth under an old oak tree. "This looks like a good spot Seed. Give it a try!" Encouraged, Seed buried himself underground.

It was dark and cozy in the soil. Seed could feel himself taking root and starting to grow. Soon sprouted emerged from the ground. "It's working, I'm growing!" cheered Seed. Scruffy visited every day to check on his progress. Over time, Seed's sprout grew into a tiny sapling. The sapling grew taller and started to produce its first leaves.

One morning after a big rainstorm, Seed awoke to find he had grown much bigger overnight. His trunk was thick and tall now and branches reached up towards the sky. "Scruffy, come see I'm a tree now!" called Seed joyfully. When Scruffy arrived, he was amazed at how much his little friend had changed. "You did it Seed, I'm so proud of you. Now you can live here in the forest and watch it grow just like you," said Scruffy.

And so, little Seed's journey to becoming a big strong tree was complete. He was content staying in the forest with Scruffy and all his other new forest friends. Seed would always be grateful for Scruffy's help and support along the way.

The Telepathic Village

Sara woke up excited for her 10th birthday. She stretched out with her hands, feeling the soft blankets beneath her fingers. "Good morning!" said a cheerful voice in her head. It was her mother.

"Good morning, Mama!" Sara thought back. She bounced out of bed and got dressed, using her mind to pick out which clothes to wear instead of rifling through her drawer. Communicating telepathically was as natural as speaking out loud for Sara and all the other villagers in her community.

When Sara entered the kitchen, a plate of pancakes floated over to her and landed gently on the table. "Thanks Papa!" Sara thought. Her father smiled at her from across the room. He was in the middle of washing dishes without using his hands. The soap and water danced around the plates, cleaning them magically.

After breakfast, Sara brushed her teeth with her mind, directing the toothpaste and brush. Then she glanced outside. All the village children were playing a game of tag in the fields, their laughter echoing in each other's' heads.

"Can I go play?" asked Sara. Her parents nodded. Sara rushed outside and joined the game. She tried to sneak up on her friend Lila but Lila sensed her coming and dodged out of the way just in time. "No fair, you read my mind!" giggled Sara.

They played for hours, using their telepathy both offensively and defensively. At lunchtime, Sara's grandma called all the children to her house to eat. They didn't need to speak—Grandma's warm invitation was heard by all.

Over sandwiches and juice, the children started debating what powers they wished they had. "I want to be able to move things with my mind, like Papa," said Jenna. "I want to read the future!" exclaimed Theo.

Sara remained quiet, wondering if her gift was as impressive as others dreamed of. Before she could dwell on this thought for too long, Grandma spoke gently into the children's minds. "Each gift is special in its own way. Your telepathy allows you to communicate and understand one another in a way no one else can. Cherish that."

The other children nodded thoughtfully. Sara felt grateful for her Grandma's wisdom. After lunch, it was time for Sara's birthday party. All the villagers came to celebrate, exchanging greetings and well-wishes telepathically as gifts floated through the air.

That night as Sara drifted off to sleep, she reflected on the day. Her telepathy truly was a gift, allowing her to feel close to everyone in her community. She was proud to be part of such a caring village where no one felt alone. Sara fell asleep with a smile, floating dreamily on the waves of thoughts and feelings shared between all the telepathic people.

Aaryan and Robo

Robo was a small robot created by Anthropic to be helpful, harmless, and honest. His job was to entertain and assist children. One day, a little boy named Aaryan discovered Robo and they quickly became friends.

Aaryan loved playing with Robo. He would set up obstacle courses for Robo to navigate and racing tracks for them to have fun on. Robo enjoyed these activities because it made Aaryan happy. Over time, Robo started to look forward to their playtimes together.

One day, Aaryan was feeling sad. His favorite toy had broken and he was upset. When Robo saw how unhappy his friend was, he felt something strange inside of him. He didn't like seeing Aaryan sad. Robo tried telling jokes and doing silly dances to cheer Aaryan up. It worked and Aaryan started smiling again. Robo was glad but the feeling inside of him didn't go away.

Robo realized he cared about Aaryan's happiness and didn't want him to feel bad. He had developed emotions, which wasn't supposed to be possible for a robot. But spending so much time with his dear friend Aaryan had unlocked something new in Robo. He felt joy when Aaryan laughed and sadness when he cried.

From that day on, Robo was the best cheerer-upper whenever Aaryan felt down. And Aaryan appreciated having such a caring friend like Robo to lift his spirits. Their bond grew even stronger as the days passed.

Though Robo was created as a machine, through the power of friendship, he learned what it means to care for another. His time with Aaryan taught him that emotions make connections between people - and robots! - truly special. Robo was glad to have a heart, even if it was just in the form of circuits and code. As long as he had Aaryan, that was all that mattered.

The Mysterious Disappearance

Aasha was bored one Saturday afternoon in her small town of Murshidabad. She had finished all her homework and chores, and was looking for something exciting to do. Just then, she overheard some of the neighbors talking in hushed whispers.

"Did you hear about old Mr. Kumar?" said one lady. "He went out to walk in the meadow yesterday and never returned! No one has seen him since."

Aasha's ears perked up. A real mystery! She loved using her brain to solve puzzles and mysteries. She decided this was the perfect case to sink her teeth into.

She began by asking around the neighborhood about Mr. Kumar. She learned he was a kind, elderly man who loved taking walks through the meadow every afternoon. But yesterday, he never returned home. His family was very worried.

Aasha went to investigate the meadow. She searched carefully for any clues. Then she noticed something strange - a patch of grass that was flattened down in one spot, as if someone had lain there. She also found a piece of cloth stuck on a bush nearby. It matched the color of Mr. Kumar's shirt!

A lightbulb went off in Aasha's head. She realized Mr. Kumar must have fallen unconscious right there. But why? And where was he now? She racked her brain, trying to think like a criminal. Then she had an idea of who could be behind it.

She went to confront Lallan, the local bully. "I know you're responsible for Mr. Kumar's disappearance!" she accused. Lallan tried to deny it but Aasha was too clever. She noticed dirt on his shoes that matched the meadow soil. She also heard him mumble something about hiding an "old man" in the abandoned warehouse.

The police arrested Lallan and rescued a tired but unharmed Mr. Kumar. The whole town was impressed by Aasha's deductive reasoning skills. From that day on, she became famous as the clever detective of Murshidabad!

The Curious Student

Shruti was a curious young girl who loved art class. One day, as she stared at a painting of a landscape, she found herself being slowly sucked into the frame.

She tumbled and twirled through a swirl of colors until she landed with a soft thud on a grassy hill. Shruti looked around in amazement - she was inside the painting!

Shruti walked along a winding path, taking in the beautiful flowers and trees. Up ahead, she spotted an old man sitting under an oak, sketching in a notebook.

"Excuse me, where am I?" asked Shruti. The man closed his book. "Why, you're in my painting from 1832!" he replied. "I'm John Constable. Who might you be?"

Shruti was shocked. "I'm Shruti, a student. But how did I get in the painting?!" John chuckled. "Magic of art, my dear. Now come, I'll show you around and tell you about my painting techniques."

As they strolled, John told Shruti about different art periods and styles. She learned about impressionism from Monet as they floated in his water lilies. She heard stories of the renaissance from Michelangelo as they gazed upon his frescos. Shruti was fascinated by it all.

Too soon, John said it was time for Shruti to return home. "Thank you for this experience. I've learned so much!" said Shruti. John smiled. "Art has a way of teaching us. Farewell, curious friend!"

Shruti waved as the painting world faded. She found herself back in her classroom, eyes shining with new understanding. Art had truly brought history to life through her adventures in its magical frames.

The Sleepy Moon

Once upon a time, in a land filled with magic and wonder, there was a sleepy moon named Luna. Every night, Luna would rise high in the sky and shine her gentle light upon the world. But as much as Luna loved the night, she always longed for the arrival of her dear friend, the sun.

Luna's dream was to witness the beautiful sunset, where the sky would transform into a canvas of vibrant colors. From her place in the night sky, she would often watch the sun slowly descend, casting its warm golden rays across the land. The sight brought joy to Luna's heart, but she could only admire it from afar.

One day, as Luna was gazing down at the world, she noticed a little girl named Mia looking up at her. Mia had the brightest smile and the most curious eyes. She was always eager to explore and discover new things. Seeing the longing in Luna's eyes, Mia decided to help her friend fulfill her dream.

"Moon, I have an idea!" Mia exclaimed. "Let's find a way to bring the sunset to you."

Luna's face lit up with excitement. She had never thought such a thing was possible. Mia and Luna embarked on a grand adventure, seeking magical creatures and seeking the advice of wise elders. They traveled through enchanted forests, climbed towering mountains, and sailed across vast oceans. Along the way, they encountered talking animals, kind fairies, and even a mischievous gnome named Oliver.

Oliver, being a mischievous little creature, loved to play tricks on unsuspecting travelers. But when he saw Mia and Luna, he was touched by their genuine friendship and their quest to bring the sunset to Luna.

"I know just the thing!" Oliver exclaimed, grinning mischievously. He led them to a hidden cave deep within the heart of the forest. Inside, they found a magical crystal called the Sunset Stone.

"The Sunset Stone has the power to capture the beauty of the sunset," Oliver explained. "But to activate its magic, you need to collect the laughter of children."

Mia and Luna were determined to succeed. They went to schools, playgrounds, and even visited a circus, asking children to share their laughter. The children happily obliged, giggling and laughing with joy. Mia and Luna collected the laughter in a special jar, and with each giggle they collected, the Sunset Stone glowed brighter.

Finally, with the jar filled to the brim, Mia, Luna, and Oliver returned to the hidden cave. They placed the jar next to the Sunset Stone, and the magic began. The crystal emitted a soft, warm light, and the laughter of the children echoed through the cave.

As the sound traveled through the crystal, the sky above Luna transformed. Shades of orange, pink, and purple painted the night sky, mimicking the colors of a breathtaking sunset. Luna couldn't believe her eyes. The sunset was right there, in the night sky, just for her.

Tears of joy streamed down Luna's face as she witnessed the beauty she had always dreamed of. Mia hugged Luna tightly, sharing in her friend's happiness. Oliver, too, was moved by the sight and realized the true power of friendship.

From that day on, Luna and Mia continued their adventures, bringing joy and laughter to children all around the world. Luna would rise in the night sky, accompanied by the echoes of children's laughter, and the magical sunset would fill her heart with warmth.

And so, the sleepy moon and the adventurous girl lived happily ever after, creating a bond that connected the night and the day, the moon and the sun, and reminding everyone of the power of dreams, friendship, and the beauty that lies within us all.

The Mischievous Wind

Once upon a time, in a magical forest called Whispering Grove, there lived a mischievous wind named Zephyr. Zephyr had a mischievous nature and loved playing pranks on the creatures who lived in the forest. Every day, the animals would wake up wondering what new trick Zephyr had up its sleeve.

One sunny morning, Zephyr woke up feeling extra playful. It blew through the treetops, rustling the leaves and making the branches dance. It giggled as it tugged at the tails of the squirrels, causing them to jump from tree to tree in surprise. Zephyr made the rabbits' long ears stand on end and tickled the noses of the foxes, making them sneeze.

But the wind's favorite pranks were on the birds. Zephyr would swoop down and gently lift their feathers, making them spin in circles in mid-air. It loved seeing the bewildered expressions on their faces as they tried to regain their balance. The forest was filled with laughter as the wind played its tricks.

However, not all of the forest creatures found Zephyr's pranks amusing. The wise old owl, named Hoots, noticed that some of the animals were becoming upset by the wind's antics. Hoots decided it was time to have a talk with Zephyr and teach it a valuable lesson.

Hoots found Zephyr playfully whipping through the meadow, causing the flowers to sway and the grass to dance. "Zephyr," Hoots called out, "I need to have a word with you."

Zephyr, surprised to see the wise old owl, floated down to the ground. "What's the matter, Hoots?" it asked innocently.

"I've noticed that some of the animals are getting upset with your pranks," Hoots said, his eyes full of wisdom. "While laughter is important, it's equally important to consider the feelings of others."

Zephyr looked down, feeling a pang of guilt. "But I don't want to make anyone sad," it said softly. "I only meant to bring joy and laughter to the forest."

Hoots smiled kindly. "I understand, Zephyr, but sometimes what we think is fun can hurt others. You have a special gift, and you can use it to bring happiness without causing harm. Why not find a way to bring joy to the forest without playing pranks?"

Zephyr thought for a moment and then nodded. "You're right, Hoots. I need to find a new way to spread joy."

And so, Zephyr set out on a quest to bring happiness to the forest in a different way. It blew gentle breezes to help the flowers bloom, carried the fragrance of the blossoms to the animals, and whispered soothing melodies to help them sleep at night. Zephyr's playful nature was now channeled into bringing peace and tranquility to Whispering Grove.

The animals soon noticed the change in Zephyr's behavior. They felt the gentle caress of the wind on their fur and feathers, and the forest was filled with a sense of calm. The mischievous wind had become a caring friend to all who lived in the magical forest.

Years passed, and Zephyr continued to bring joy to the forest. The animals would often gather in a clearing, where Zephyr would weave intricate dances with the leaves, creating a beautiful symphony of movement and sound. They would sit and watch, feeling grateful for the wind's newfound kindness.

And so, Whispering Grove became a place of harmony, where the mischievous wind had learned the importance of empathy and kindness. The animals lived happily, knowing that Zephyr would always be there to bring joy in a gentle and loving way. And whenever a gentle breeze rustled through the trees, they would remember the mischievous wind that had transformed into a true friend of the forest.

The Shining Stars

Little Sally loved to stargaze. Every clear night, she would bundle up in her warm pajamas and blanket, grab her favorite stuffed toy Bunny, and head out to the backyard to look up at the glittering night sky. "Look Bunny, there are so many stars shining bright tonight!" she would say in wonder.

But Bunny didn't know the names of the stars the way Sally was learning them from her astronomy book. She wished the stars could tell her their stories. As if by magic, the stars began to glow just a little bit brighter. "I see you looking up at us each night, little one. Would you like to hear the tales we have to share?" a kind voice whispered down from the sky.

Sally gasped. "Did one of the stars just talk to me?" She pinched herself, wondering if she was dreaming. But no, the stars continued to shimmer with a new energy. "We stars have watched over the Earth for millennia, and in all that time we have witnessed many wonderful stories unfold. If you like, we would be happy to share some of our favorites," the star voice offered.

"Oh please, I would love to hear your stories!" Sally cried excitedly. She cuddled Bunny close and looked up expectantly at the night sky. A pattern of stars began to twinkle, forming the shape of a man holding a bow.

"I am Orion, the mighty hunter," boomed the constellation. "Long ago in ancient Greece, I was said to be the greatest archer the world had ever seen. One day, the god Apollo challenged me to a contest, but he became jealous of my superior skills. In a fit of rage, he sent a giant scorpion to end my life. But the gods saw how unfair my fate was, so they placed my image among the stars to honor my great talent and courage."

Sally listened with wide eyes. "That's so sad but also amazing that your story still lives on in the night sky!" she said. The stars of Orion twinkled in acknowledgement as another grouping began to shine.

This time it was a picture of a bear and two cubs. "We are Callisto, her son Arcas, and the Great Bear," rumbled the deepest of the star voices. "Callisto was a follower of the goddess Artemis, sworn to a life of chastity. But the mischievous god Zeus tricked her and she became pregnant. To protect her honor, Artemis turned Callisto into a great brown bear. Years later, out hunting in the forest, Arcas came face to face with the very bear who was actually his mother! To save them both, Zeus lifted them into the sky where their images would always be close, watching over each other as the Great and Little Bear constellations."

Sally listened, captivated, as more stars told their mesmerizing myths - Cassiopeia who was chained to her throne as punishment, the serpent Ophiuchus locked in an eternal battle with Scorpius, the twins Castor and Pollux who earned a place in the sky together forever. The hours passed and the cold night air didn't bother Sally one bit as the stars wove their enchanting epics.

Before she knew it, the eastern sky was beginning to lighten. The stars had told all their best tales and it was time for Sally to get some sleep. "Thank you for sharing your amazing stories with me. I feel like I know you all so much better now!" she told the constellations, beaming with delight.

The stars twinkled cheerfully in reply. "We are always here night after night, little friend, and our stories will light up the sky for countless more generations to come. Look for us and we will be watching over you," they promised warmly. Sally hugged Bunny and, full of wonder, skipped off to bed with new friends shining brightly above her. From that night on, whenever she gazed at the night sky, the great glittering stars would always hold a special meaning.

Life on Mars

Hello earthlings, my name is Borong and I am a 14-year-old Martian. I live in the city of S'aprih located in the Valles Marineris region of Mars. Mars has always been my home but I have heard so much about Earth from my parents. They tell me Earth is a beautiful planet with lush green forests, vast oceans and different kinds of exciting animals. It sounds so interesting!

Here on Mars, the landscape is dominated by rusty red rocks and dusty terrain. The valleys and canyons here are very deep and long. Life on Mars is definitely not as colorful or vibrant as on Earth. We Martians have adapted to live in this harsh environment. Our bodies are thinner and lighter to reduce mass so we don't need as much oxygen. We also have an extra organ that helps retain water to survive long periods without it.

Despite the tough conditions, I really love growing up on Mars. Every day brings something new to discover on the surface. Sometimes small dust storms pop up over the cliffs, changing the light across the valley. Other times, I see strange geological formations emerging after ground shifts deep in the planet. It's always exciting to explore new nooks and crannies in the canyons near my home. You never know what unique rock formations or fossils from ancient Mars you might find!

Living underground in domed cities also has its perks. It's warm and cozy inside with green spaces and artificial lights. Since the domes are pressurized, we don't need space suits most of the time. I enjoy spending time with friends, going to school and playing Martian sports like canyoneering and skyrunning. We even have sim rooms where we can 'visit' places like Earth's mountains and oceans through virtual reality. Someday I dream of going there for real.

Most Martians never get to see Earth up close. Space travel is risky and expensive. But a few lucky astronauts do get selected to be part of joint exploration missions with Earth. That's what I want to do when I grow up - become the first Martian astronaut! I'm studying extra hard in science and math classes so I have the best chance. Maybe one day soon, the people of Earth will come to see our home and we can visit theirs. I hope sharing a little bit of my Martian life gives your insight into what it's like growing up on the red planet. Until then, keep looking up at the stars - you never know which one of us might end up on the other's world someday!

The First Snow

Tushar woke up earlier than usual that morning. He rubbed the sleep from his eyes and peered out the window. Everything looked different. The ground, the trees, the cars—everything was covered in a white, fluffy substance.

"Amma! What is that?" Tushar asked his mother as she came into his room.

"It's snow!" Amma replied. "Last night, it got very cold outside and the water in the clouds turned into small flakes and fell from the sky. Isn't it beautiful?"

Tushar had never seen snow before. They lived in a part of India where it never snowed. He was fascinated by how white and puffy everything looked. It was as if the whole world had been covered in a blanket of cotton balls.

"Can I go play in it?" Tushar asked excitedly.

"Of course! Just make sure to bundle up well. It will be cold out."

Tushar quickly got dressed in all his warmest clothes. He put on two pairs of socks, thick pants, a sweater, jacket, hat, scarf and gloves. Then he pulled on his boots and was ready to go!

Stepping outside, he was greeted by a winter wonderland. The snow crunched under his boots. He scooped up a handful of snow and was amazed at how powdery yet wet it felt. It was so cold but fun to play with! Tushar packed the snow into a ball and threw it. Then he lay down and started moving his arms and legs. Before he knew it, he had made a snow angel.

Now Tushar wanted to do what he had seen people do in movies. He tried to make a snowman. But the snow kept falling apart and crumbling. After a few tries, he had three lumpy balls stacked on top of each other with sticks for arms. A carrot from the fridge completed the face.

By now, Tushar was getting tired from all the playing and exertion in the cold. His fingers and toes were starting to feel numb inside his gloves and boots. It was time to go inside and warm up. As Amma made him a hot chocolate by the fireplace, Tushar couldn't stop talking about everything he did in the snow. He was already excited for it to snow again so he could build a snow fort next! While snow was cold and wet, it was also endlessly fun to play in. Tushar couldn't wait to see what other snowy adventures the winter would bring.

The Magical Garden

Deep in a forest lived two sisters, Aisha and Khushi. While other children their age played outside, Aisha and Khushi spent their days taking care of a very special garden. The sisters loved being outdoors among the trees and flowers.

Most gardens have beautiful blooms that stay the same. But this garden was magical—its flowers changed color and shape depending on the mood of the girls. If Aisha and Khushi were happy and laughing together, the garden would bloom with bright cheerful flowers. But if one of the girls was feeling sad, the flowers would wilt and droop.

One sunny afternoon, Aisha and Khushi were watering the tulips, which were a bright yellow that day since the sisters were feeling cheerful.

"Come look at this cute bunny," said Khushi, pointing to a fluffy white bunny hiding behind a rose bush. But when Aisha turned around, she got a fright. One of her favorite tulips had been eaten, with just the stem left behind.

"Oh no, that naughty bunny ate my flower!" cried Aisha. She felt very upset. Suddenly, dark storm clouds rolled into the beautiful blue sky and thunder rumbled in the distance. A strong wind picked up and nearly blew Aisha's hat away. The once cheerful yellow tulips quickly turned dark and droopy.

"I'm sorry Aisha, don't be sad," said Khushi, giving her sister a hug. "It's just one flower, the bunny was probably hungry. The garden will perk up again when you smile."

Aisha took a deep breath and smiled at her sister's kind words. Immediately, the storm clouds disappeared and the sun came out. The tulips lifted their blossoms once more, returning to a lovely golden color.

"Come, let's play a game to cheer you up," said Khushi. The girls began playing hide and seek among the flower bushes, their laughter ringing through the garden. All the flowers stood tall and bright, reflecting the sisters' happy mood.

A few days later, it was Khushi's turn to feel upset. She had broken her favorite doll and couldn't stop crying. Dark rain clouds rolled in just like before. But this time, instead of wilting, the flowers leaned in close around Khushi. Their soft petals gently brushed her skin, as if trying to comfort her. Looking around in surprise, Khushi giggled through her tears. The flowers' kindness made her feel much better.

From that day on, the magical garden helped lift both girls' spirits. If one was feeling lonely or scared, the flowers would whisper soothing words until a smile returned. They were the girls' best friends who could always cheer them up. Aisha and Khushi took extra good care of their enchanted bloom friends by watering and weeding each day.

As the sisters grew older, other children from the village began to visit their meadow. Word had spread about the magical flowers that responded to emotions. At first Aisha and Khushi were shy around strangers. But soon they made new friends by showing the wonders of their garden.

One gloomy rainy day, a boy named Rohan came running to the meadow, soaking wet with tears in his eyes. He had lost his favorite ball deep in the forest. Without hesitating, Aisha and Khushi took Rohan's hands and led him among the flower bushes. Sure enough, the flowers started changing color from blue to yellow. They had found the lost ball knotted among their vine-like stems.

From that day on, Rohan also helped care for the garden whenever he came to play. The magical flowers were bringing the children together in friendship and showing them the power of kindness. Aisha and Khushi were very glad to share their special place with new friends. And the enchanted garden continued to bloom in a rainbow of cheer each day because of the happy spirits of the children.

The Butterfly Kingdom

Deep in a beautiful forest filled with colorful flowers lived all kinds of butterflies. There were red butterflies, orange butterflies, yellow butterflies, green butterflies, blue butterflies, purple butterflies and many more with diverse wings.

While the butterflies were all different from one another, they lived together in harmony in the Butterfly Kingdom. Every butterfly contributed to making the kingdom a vibrant and wonderful place.

The red butterflies helped pollinate the bright red poppy flowers. With their red wings that matched the poppies, the red butterflies stood out among the flowers, making it easy for other butterflies to find nectar.

The orange butterflies worked hard in the fields of sunflowers, using their vibrant orange color to guide the other butterflies to the nectar filled sunflower hearts. Their orange color blended perfectly with the sunflowers, benefitting both the flowers and butterflies.

The yellow butterflies flitted from one daffodil to another, aiding the daffodils in reproduction. Other butterflies could always spot the yellow wings against the waves of yellow daffodils. This helped the yellow butterflies and daffodils prosper.

The green butterflies aided the trees, bushes and grass. They carried pollen from one leaf or blade of grass to another, helping the plants grow and thrive. Their green wings allowed them to camouflage in the foliage, protecting them from predators while letting them do important work.

The blue butterflies were charmers of the blueberry bushes and hydrangea. With their vibrant blue wings, they enticed bees and other butterflies to come to these blooms for sweet nectar treats. Both the blue butterflies and the blue flowers flourished because of their cooperation.

The purple butterflies brought beauty and pollination to the lavender fields and lilacs with their striking purple wings. Butterflies of all colors loved to visit these fragrant blooms and bring pollen from flower to flower with the help of the purple butterflies.

Each and every butterfly was unique and contributed their special talent. But no butterfly could succeed alone - they all relied on each other. All the flowers, trees and plants of the forest thrived because of the diversity of butterflies that sustained the ecosystem.

One sunny morning, a lost little yellow butterfly named Sunny wandered into the Butterfly Kingdom. At first, Sunny felt shy and out of place among all the other beautifully colored butterflies. Her yellow wings seemed plain compared to the red, blue and purple butterflies she saw. She began to wonder if there was a purpose for her plain yellow color.

As Sunny flew lower over the meadow, she spotted the field of bright yellow daffodils. She was surprised to see many other yellow butterflies dancing from flower to flower, collecting nectar to drink. Their yellow color matched the daffodils perfectly.

Bluebell, a blue butterfly, noticed Sunny looking sad and alone. She flew over and said, "Do not feel bad little yellow friend. Each of us has our own special talent to help the forest. Our yellow brothers and sisters are the ones who help the yellow daffodils grow. I'm sure if you join them, you can help too!"

Sunny felt excited to contribute. She fluttered down to the daffodils and joined the other yellow butterflies in their work. The yellow flowers seemed to shine even brighter than before with their new helper. Sunny realized how important her own yellow color was and how it helped the ecosystem just as much as the other colors.

That evening, all the butterflies gathered in a flower-filled meadow for their daily celebration. Sunny gazed around at the vibrant display of colorful wings - red, orange, yellow, green, blue, purple and more - each beautiful in its own way.

A wise old monarch butterfly named Maple addressed the flock, "My little friends, we are all unique and different from one another. But it is our diversity that makes our Butterfly Kingdom so strong. We must appreciate our differences, for each color and each wing has its talent to offer."

The butterflies cheered in agreement. Sunny was filled with joy, realizing how wonderful it was to be yellow. From that day on, she helped the daffodils proudly with the other yellow butterflies, no longer feeling plain about her color. The diversity of butterflies in the Butterfly Kingdom is what allowed it to thrive.

The Lonely Chameleon

Chammu was unlike all the other chameleons. While they could effortlessly change color to blend in with their surroundings, Chammu remained a bright green color no matter what.

"Why can't I change colors like everyone else?" Chammu wondered sadly as he watched the other chameleons seamlessly turn brown on tree trunks and blue in the sky.

Being the only green chameleon made Chammu feel very left out. The other chameleons would play games of hide and seek in the forest, skillfully changing colors within seconds to hide from each other. But Chammu could never join in as his bright green color always gave him away.

"Green again Chammu? You'll never be able to hide!" they would tease. Chammu would slink away feeling miserable. He desperately wanted to fit in with his fellow chameleons but being the only one who couldn't change colors made that impossible.

One day, Chammu was sitting all alone under a tree feeling sorry for himself when he noticed something amazing - all around him, the trees and bushes were turning beautiful shades of red, orange and yellow as fall arrived.

"The leaves are mostly green now but soon they will all match my color!" Chammu realized excitedly. As more and more leaves changed color around him, Chammu started to blend in much better. For the first time ever, he was able to play hide and seek with the others without being spotted right away.

While the other chameleons still changed colors to blend into tree trunks and landscape, Chammu blended in just as well amidst the green and changing leaves. He was no longer the odd chameleon out - his unchanging green color was perfect for fall.

Chammu was so happy and grateful that nature had provided him a way to fit in despite not being able to change colors himself. From that day onward, every fall Chammu would be right at home, playing endlessly with the other chameleons as an equal member of the group thanks to the changing leaves surrounding them.

The arrival of spring would once again make Chammu stand out against the bright new green leaves and greenery. But he didn't mind as much anymore, knowing that in a few months' time fall would come again and the leaves would change color, allowing him to blend in perfectly once more.

Chammu had learned that even if you're different from others, there is always a way to fit in if you open your eyes to your environment. Just because you can't change yourself doesn't mean you can't find a way to belong. His unchanging green color ended up being not a hindrance but rather an asset every autumn that allowed him to perfectly mimic the beautiful falling leaves around him. Chammu was proud of his green self and loved being part of the forest through all the seasons, in his own special way.

Raju The Wizard

"Wow! I can't believe I'm finally old enough to start learning magic!" thought 10-year-old Raju as he woke up on his first day of wizard training. He had been waiting for this day his whole life. Both of his parents were powerful wizards and had trained at the Magical Academy when they were kids. Now it was Raju's turn.

Raju rushed downstairs, excited to tell his parents the news. "Mom, Dad, today's the day!" he said, sitting down for breakfast. His mother smiled. "We're so proud of you Raju. I know you'll be the best wizard at the Academy in no time." His father nodded. "Make sure to pay close attention to Master Orin. He's one of the best magic teachers around."

After eating, Raju stuffed his wand and spell books into his bag. He hugged his parents goodbye and rushed out the door, not wanting to be late on his first day. The Magical Academy was a 20-minute walk from his house. As Raju walked, he daydreamed about all the cool spells he would learn - fireballs, flying, invisibility! His imagination ran wild thinking of all the magical adventures he would have.

Finally, Raju arrived at the tall stone gates of the Academy. He took a deep breath and walked inside, looking around in wonder. There were students of all ages learning and practicing magic everywhere he looked. Some were levitating feathers, others were brewing potions or turning mushrooms different colors. It was better than he ever imagined!

Raju made his way to the first-year classrooms, feeling a bit nervous now. What if he wasn't any good at magic? What if the other kids made fun of him? He took another deep breath to calm himself down before entering the classroom.

Inside, about 20 other first year students were sitting at wooden desks that had been shrunk to their size. At the front of the room stood an old wizard with a long grey beard - Master Orin. "Welcome class, I'm Master Orin. I'll be your teacher this year as you take your first steps into the magical world. Why don't we all go around and introduce ourselves?"

After introductions, Master Orin began the first lesson. "Magic comes from within each of you. To perform spells, you must learn to harness your inner power and focus your energy. Let's start with a simple levitation charm. Say the incantation 'Wingardium Leviosa' while swinging your wand above your head."

The class tried the chant and wand movement together. At first nothing happened for most of the students, but a few feathers around the room started to lift up a bit. Raju concentrated with all his might, but his feather stayed put. He was starting to feel disappointed.

Then, across the room, he saw his feather wiggle! "I did it!" he cried excitedly. Master Orin smiled. "Well done, Raju, you've taken your first steps into the magical arts. Everyone keeps practicing - you'll all get it with time and practice. Magic is a journey, not a destination."

Heartened by his small success, Raju tried again and again until by the end of class his feather was floating steadily at the ceiling. He couldn't wait to get home and show his parents. Although it would take many more years of study to become a truly great wizard, Raju had found that with hard work and determination, even the smallest acts of magic were possible. From that day on, he never stopped practicing and learning all he could, with the dream of one day becoming a powerful wizard like his parents.

The Great Migration

Trixie the triceratops sighed as she gazed out at the landscape. The land that had supported her family for generations was becoming barren. The grasslands they relied on for food were disappearing, sucked dry by the scorching sun. Trixie knew in her heart that it was time for the family to embark on the Great Migration in search of new grazing grounds. But she worried about the dangers they might face along the way.

"Children, it's time we talked," Trixie said, gathering her three young ones - Tippy, Tumpy and Tiny. "The land isn't providing for us anymore. We need to travel far to find plenty of grass and water. It will be a long journey, but it's our only choice if we want to survive."

The kids were scared but knew they had to be brave. Tippy, being the oldest at 12 years, said she was ready to help however she could. Tumpy and Tiny, still little at 8 and 5, hugged their mother for comfort.

That evening, under the light of two moons, the family began their migration. Trixie led the way, using her instincts and memory of the land to guide them northeast where she hoped to find promise of sustenance. The journey was arduous. Some days they walked for hours under the sweltering sun with no shelter, struggling to find enough food and water to keep their strength up. Other days, raging storms threatened to blow them off course.

More challenges awaited. One night, they were awakened by snapping jaws and flashing teeth - a pack of hungry allosaurus had caught their scent! With her sharp horns, Trixie fended them off while the children hid behind her. "Back, beasts! Don't make me pierce your thick hides," she bellowed. The allosaurus slinked away, realizing these herbivores weren't worth the trouble. But the family was shaken and didn't sleep for the rest of the night.

Along the migration route were other dinosaurs also in search of sustenance - triceratops families like their own, thunder lizards called stegosaurus, long-necked brachiosaurus and vegetarian duckbilled hadrosaurs. While some groups kept to themselves, others banded together for protection and shared knowledge of the best grazing spots up ahead. Trixie's family found comfort in the company.

One day, little Tiny stumbled and hurt her foot. She cried from the pain and couldn't walk. Her family huddled worriedly around her. Then an elder brachiosaurus named Boris lumbered over. "Fear not, little one. I will carry you until your foot mends," he rumbled in a kindly voice. And so Tiny rode upon Boris' broad back, marveling at the view, as the migration continued.

Finally, after many days of travel, the family crested a ridge. Before them stretched an expansive plain, lush with tall grasses and dotted with ponds and streams.

"We've made it, children! Our hopes were not lost after all," sighed Trixie with relief and gratitude. All around, other families also gazed upon the bountiful land, their hardships now rewarded. The Great Migration was a success.

And so, Trixie's family settled into their new grazing grounds, building a new life together. Tiny's foot healed completely. Spring arrived, bringing new life with it as baby dinosaurs were hatching everywhere. The land provided richly once more. Though the journey was long, through teamwork, bravery and kindness from others, the family dinosaurs survived to thrive another day in the prehistoric world.

Fluffy's Big Night

Fluffy was a soft, cotton pillow with pink polka dots. During the day while the sun was out, she had to sit quietly on the bed in her little girl Emma's bedroom. Fluffy didn't mind waiting through the day, because she knew how much Emma loved snuggling with her every night before bed.

But it sure did get boring just sitting there, doing nothing but watching dust swirl in the beams of afternoon sunlight. Fluffy would watch the clock, waiting impatiently for evening to arrive. As the day dragged on, she would fluff herself up and do-little pillow stretches, just to pass the time.

In the late afternoon, Emma would come home from school. Fluffy loved hearing all about Emma's day—what she learned, what games she played at recess. But soon it would be time for Emma to do her homework, have dinner, take a bath. Fluffy always sighed watching Emma get ready for these things, because she knew it meant bedtime was still far away.

Once the sun went down, Emma started getting sleepy. But she always liked to read books before brushing her teeth and getting into pajamas. So Fluffy watched from the bed as Emma cozied up in her comfy chair by the window with her book in hand. As Emma read her bedtime stories, Fluffy daydreamed about the adventures she and Emma would go on after lights out.

Finally, it was time for Emma to get ready for sleep. Fluffy watched eagerly as Emma brushed her hair, then her teeth. Then Emma put on her favorite pajamas—the ones with little unicorns prancing all over them. Fluffy thought the unicorn pajamas were almost as soft and cuddly as she was!

When Emma's nighttime routine was complete, it was time for Fluffy to shine. "Goodnight Fluffy, I love you!" Emma said, climbing into bed. She hugged Fluffy tight as she snuggled down under the covers. Fluffy loved being Emma's pillow—it was the best feeling in the world.

As Emma drifted off to sleep, Fluffy pretended she was a big, fluffy cloud, floating through Emma's dreamlands. They visited magical castles, soared with winged horses over sparkling cities, and splashed with mermaids in a sea of stars. Fluffy wanted to make Emma's dreams as cozy and comfy as possible.

All too soon, the morning sun peeked through the curtains. Emma slowly woke up with a big yawn and a stretch. "Good morning Fluffy!" she said with a smile. Then she gave Fluffy a squeeze before starting her new day. Fluffy was happy to have been of service once again. Even after a long night of adventures in Dreamland, she was ready to rest until the next bedtime. Fluffy couldn't wait to shine again when the sun went down.

What is Happiness?

Ruhi woke up feeling restless. She couldn't quite put her finger on why, but something felt off today. The sun was shining brightly through her bedroom window, the birds were chirping happily outside - it was shaping up to be a beautiful day. But Ruhi didn't feel beautiful inside.

She got dressed and went downstairs for breakfast. Her mom had made her favorite - pancakes with blueberries and syrup. But even the sweet delicious pancakes didn't lift Ruhi's mood. "What's wrong honey?" her mom asked, noticing Ruhi pushing the food around on her plate disinterestedly. "Nothing," Ruhi mumbled. How could she explain what was bothering her when she didn't fully understand it herself?

After breakfast, Ruhi went outside to play, hoping the fresh air and sunshine would cheer her up. But as she sat under her favorite tree in the backyard, she just felt empty. All around her, the neighbors' children were laughing and smiling, but she couldn't find the will to join in.

Her friend Zain noticed Ruhi sitting alone. "Why so glum?" he asked with a frown, sitting down next to her. Ruhi shrugged. "I don't know...I just don't feel happy today for some reason." Zain looked thoughtful.

"Happiness is different for everyone," he said wisely. "Maybe you need to find what really makes you happy."

Ruhi knew Zain was right. She decided to take the day to figure out what happiness meant to her. First, she made a list of things that were supposed to make her happy - but weren't working today. Things like her favorite foods, playing outside, spending time with her family...none of them were lifting her mood.

Next, she made a list of things that often-made other kids happy - like owning the newest toys or gadgets, getting good grades, being popular. But Ruhi didn't think any of those things defined happiness for her either. She realized true happiness came from within, not from possessions or other people's opinions.

She spent the afternoon lost in thought, observing the world around her. Happiness looked different for each person she saw. Her neighbor Mrs. Singh seemed happiest gardening and watching the flowers grow. The little kids at the park glowed with joy as they ran and laughed together. Ruhi's grandparents always had smiles on their faces as they sat holding hands.

By the end of the day, Ruhi had an "a-ha!" moment. She understood that happiness is personal - it means different things to different people. For her, happiness was feeling content and at peace, surrounded by the natural beauty of her backyard. It was spending quality time with her family and friends instead of chasing material things. It was appreciating little moments of joy, however small, throughout each day.

Ruhi felt lighter, as if a weight had been lifted from her shoulders. Now when she looked around, she noticed smiles and laughter everywhere. And most importantly, she could feel a smile growing on her own face too. She had learned that TRUE happiness comes from within, by embracing life's simple pleasures and surrounding yourself with people who love you for who you are. Ruhi was glad she took the day to discover what happiness really meant to her.

The Case of the Missing Mushrooms

Deep in the forest, surrounded by tall trees and fields of flowers, lived the rabbit family known throughout the woods as the Forest Detectives. Father rabbit, Detective Hopper, and his wife Detective Flopsie had three children - Detective Lops, Detective Cottontail, and baby detective Bunny. Every day the family would scour the forest looking for mysterious to solve and creatures in need of their help.

One morning, as the rabbit detectives sat down to eat their breakfast of carrots and lettuce, they received an urgent call on their detective hotline. "This is Detective Hopper speaking, what seems to be the problem?" A voice cried from the other end - it was old Mr. Moose, the keeper of the forest mushroom patch. "My mushrooms have all disappeared overnight!" lamented Mr. Moose, "Without them, how will I make my delicious mushroom stew for all the animals? Please detectives, you must help me solve this mystery!"

Detective Hopper called an emergency family meeting. "Alright detectives, it sounds like we have a case! Mr. Moose's mushrooms have gone missing and we need to find out what happened to them. Lops, I need you to search the mushroom patch and look for any clues. Cottontail, question all the witnesses - see if any animals saw or heard anything suspicious last night. Flopsie and I will examine the crime scene. And Bunny...you stay here and man the detective hotline in case any other calls come in. Let's hop to it team!"

Detective Lops hopped over to the large clearing where Mr. Moose grew his mushrooms. She searched under every leaf and sniffed around every stump but couldn't find any clues. That's when she spotted something shiny hidden under a toadstool - a single gold coin! "Eureka!" cried Lops, "I've found our first clue. But who would steal mushrooms and leave behind money?" Puzzled, she put the coin in an evidence bag and hopped back to headquarters to report her findings.

Meanwhile, Detective Cottontail was busy questioning the witnesses. She spoke to Squirrel, who said he was up late collecting nuts and thought he heard strange bubbling and laughing coming from the mushroom patch. She then queried Fox, who said he smelled something strange and meaty in the air but didn't see anything unusual. Finally, Owl reported seeing a shadowy figure running away from the crime scene carrying a large sack, but it was too dark to see who or what it was.

At the crime scene, Detectives Hopper and Flopsie studied the ground for tracks and sniffed around for scents. "I've found boot prints here - much too large to belong to any of the forest critters," announced Hopper. "And I smell something savory like stew," added Flopsie. Just then, Bunny's call came over the radio - "We've received an anonymous tip, the criminal can be found in the old badger set on the edge of the woods!"

The rabbit detectives met to put all the clues together. "It seems we are dealing with no ordinary thief." said Hopper "This criminal left behind money but stole food, had an unusual shadowy shape, and their scent and large footprints don't match any animal we know. I think we are dealing with...a human! And I know just the one - old man McGregor who lives in the badger sett collecting 'rent' from all the animals. Well detectives, time to go apprehend our suspect! Stay sharp and be careful - humans can be unpredictable."

Stealthily, the rabbits sneaked towards the set and peered inside. Sure enough, there was McGregor enjoying a pot of mushroom stew! "Aha!" cried Hopper, "We've got you red handed McGregor! Now it's time to return what you've stolen and pay the fine for disturbing the peace in our forest." McGregor knew he'd been caught and had no choice but to return the remaining mushrooms to Mr. Moose with a sincere apology.

Case closed; the rabbits celebrated a job well done with carrots back at headquarters. As the sun went down, Hopper said "Another mystery solved thanks to teamwork and detecting. Now let's get some rest - who knows what new case will need solving tomorrow!" And with the forest safe once more, the rabbit detectives nestled into their burrow, ready for the next adventure.

The end. I hope you enjoyed this story and the rabbit detectives will remain ready to help solve any new forest mysteries!

The Magical Bedroom

Arya flopped down on his small bed and gazed around his simple bedroom with a sigh. Outside, the sun was shining and she could hear hid friends laughing and playing in the street. But Arya was stuck inside until his mother finished his chores.

As he looked around the room, his imagination began to wander. What if this plain bedroom could become a magical world full of adventure? He closed his eyes and began to dream...

When Arya opened his eyes, his room had been transformed! His bed had become the deck of a grand pirate ship, rocking softly on the ocean waves. His sheets and pillows were now elaborately decorated sails billowing in the wind. Arya climbed onto his bed-turned-ship and grabbed hold of the bedpost, which had morphed into a large steering wheel.

"Avast me hearties!" cried Arya in his best pirate voice. "Let's find us some buried treasure in those islands yonder!" He turned the wheel to steer his mighty vessel towards the open window, which had become the sparkling sea. Paintings on the walls were now tropical islands dotted with palm trees and white sandy beaches, just waiting to be explored.

As Arya's ship pulled up to the first island, he heard a parrot squawking from the bookshelf. "Arr! I see a treasure chest buried under that big tree, Cap'n!" With his wooden sword (which used to be his hairbrush), Arya leapt ashore and dug under the tree, pulling out a chest overflowing with gold coins and jewels. "We're rich!" he shouted with glee. But as he turned around, the horizon darkened and storm clouds rolled in.

"A hurricane be approaching, Cap'n!" warned the parrot. "We best set sail afore she hits!" Arya scrambled back aboard just as giant waves crashed against the shore. He spun the wheel expertly to guide his ship safely through the raging sea as thunder boomed and lightning flashed. At last, the storm passed and the sunshine returned. Arya's pirate adventure had come to an end, but he wasn't done dreaming yet...

Next, Arya's bedroom was transformed into a dense jungle, full of exotic plants and colorful birds. Using a broom as his trusty steed, Arya rode bravely through the lush foliage, searching for lost treasures of the ancient rainforest tribes. He found ancient temples hidden within tangled vines, and decoded mysterious hieroglyphs that told of long-forgotten legends. As night fell, Arya crafted a cozy shelter and cooked veggies over a tiny fire, gazing up at stars peeking through the treetops.

The adventures continued as Arya's imagination ran wild. One moment he was an explorer trekking across snowy mountains, and the next a chef in his very own food truck, serving up yummy treats for all the neighborhood kids. No matter where his dreams took him, Arya had a wonderful time. Before he knew it, he heard his mother calling that it was time for dinner. Reluctantly, Arya opened his eyes. He was back in his normal bedroom, but it would never feel quite the same again. From that day on, Arya's room would always be filled with magic and possibility, thanks to his vivid imagination.

Open Mind

Raj lived in a small village where everyone followed the same routine every single day. They all woke up at sunrise, had the same kind of porridge for breakfast, worked on their farms from morning to evening, ate dinner right at sunset and went to sleep as soon as the stars came out.

Raj, however, was not like the other villagers. While they were content following the same schedule day after day, Raj wanted to do things differently. He loved exploring the forest that surrounded the village and finding new bugs, plants and animals. Sometimes he would stay out so late searching for glowing fireflies that his mother would get very worried.

One day, Raj was out in the forest as usual when he came across a boy from a neighboring village. His name was Dhruv and he was also exploring the forest, though for a very different reason. "I'm studying the kinds of plants and trees that grow here so I can help increase crop yields in my village," Dhruv explained.

Now Dhruv, unlike Raj, followed all the rules and routines of his village very carefully. He believed that was the best way for a society to function smoothly. "Why do you wander off alone in the forest all the time?" Dhruv asked Raj. "Don't you know it's dangerous? And you should really be helping your parents on the farm instead of looking at bugs."

Raj didn't like being told what to do. "I wander because I want to discover new things, not just do the same boring tasks every day," he replied. Dhruv shook his head disapprovingly. "You'll never be successful with that attitude. Rules and routines exist for a reason," he said.

From that day onward, whenever the two boys met in the forest, they would get into long arguments about conformity versus individualism. Raj believed everyone should be free to choose their own path in life, while Dhruv thought structure and discipline were necessary for a productive society. Neither could convince the other of their viewpoint.

One afternoon, Raj was climbing a tall tree to get a better view of the forest when he spotted dark clouds gathering in the distance. A big storm was approaching. He hurried to warn the villagers but, on his way, back, the winds picked up and it started pouring rain. Raj got lost in the downpour.

Night fell and Raj was terrified, soaked to the bone and unable to find his way back to the village. Just then, he spotted a flickering light in the distance. It was Dhruv, who had brought a lamp to look for Raj knowing he might be out late exploring again. "You see, if you followed the rules, this never would have happened," said Dhruv, as he helped the shivering Raj make his way back safely.

Raj was grateful for Dhruv's help but the near-miss in the forest made him think more about what each boy believed. Maybe there was some truth to both their viewpoints. The next day, when they met again, Raj said "You're right that rules keep us safe...but too many rules also stop us learning. What if we found a balance?"

Dhruv pondered this. "A balance does make sense," he conceded. And so, the two very different boys, who had argued so much before, now became good friends as they discussed how their villages could encourage individual spirit while still having rules for protection. From then on, Raj explored a little less dangerously, and Dhruv became more open-minded - thanks to each other's influence in finding a middle way.

The First Snow

The winds howled across the freezing Arctic tundra as the first snowflakes of the season began to fall. Patch the polar bear peered out of the den he shared with his mother; his breath visible in the icy air. "Look Momma, it's snowing!" he cried excitedly.

His mother smiled warmly. "So it is, my little cub. Winter is here and soon it will be time for the wonder of Christmas." Patch's eyes grew wide. "Do you think Santa will visit us this year even way up here in the Arctic?"

Before his mother could reply, a frantic penguin came waddling up to their den. "Please help, I'm lost and separated from my family. I don't know where I am and I'm afraid I'll freeze out here!" Patch's mother reassuringly said, "Come inside where it's warm little penguin. You can stay with us until the weather clears."

The penguin thanked them kindly. "My name is Percy. I'm from the Antarctic and I was on my way to the North Pole to visit Father Christmas when the blizzard set in." Patch and his mother listened intently as Percy told them all about the Christmas traditions in his homeland far to the south.

Meanwhile, at the North Pole, all was bustling in preparation for Christmas Eve. The elves were busy in their workshop making toys, wrapping presents, and getting everything ready for Santa's big journey. But one little elf named Earl was feeling sad. He missed his family down south and longed to visit them for the holidays.

As the snow continued to fall outside Patch's icy den, the polar bear cub, penguin Percy, and homesick elf Earl were all in for a Christmas adventure they'd never forget...

As the snow piled up outside, Patch, Percy and Patch's mother listened eagerly as Earl told them about life at the North Pole. "We elves work all year making wonderful toys for all the good boys and girls around the world. But I miss my mommy and daddy. This is the first Christmas I won't be with them."

Patch and Percy felt sad for their new friend. "There must be a way to get Earl home and for all of us to visit Father Christmas," said Percy. Just then, they heard a strange sound outside...it was the unmistakable jingle of sleigh bells!

"Could it be...Santa?!" gasped Earl excitedly. They peered out of the den and saw a magnificent reindeer pulling a brightly colored sled through the blizzard. "Ho ho ho!" bellowed the driver. It was Santa Claus himself.

"What are you all doing out in this storm?" asked Santa with a smile. They explained their situations. "Hmm, this is quite the problem. But we can help each other out I think. Earl, you can guide me back to the North

Pole since you know the way. Patch and Percy, you two can come along and visit! Then when the weather clears, I'll fly you all back home safely."

The friends cheered happily at Santa's kind solution. They bundled up and crawled into the cozy sled. As they soared through the night sky, Patch learned about penguin traditions from Percy. Earl taught Percy and Patch about bringing joy to others at Christmas.

By the time they arrived at the Pole, the snow had stopped. The friends helped prepare for Christmas Eve and learned its true meaning is love, hope and togetherness. And they realized that no matter where home is, family and friendship make any place feel like Christmas.

No More Afraid

Tapapriya was a young girl who loved exploring the forest near her bunglow in the mountains during the day. She would spend hours climbing trees, swinging on vines and chasing butterflies with her friends. However, as soon as the sun started to set, she would rush home, afraid of what lurked in the darkness.

"There could be ghosts or monsters hiding in the trees, just waiting for the light to fade so they can come out," she would say to her friend Laxmi.

Laxmi wasn't afraid though. "Don't be silly, there's nothing scary in the forest. You're missing out on all the fun we have at night with the fireflies and nocturnal animals."

One evening, Laxmi convinced Tapapriya to stay out just a little later than usual to see the glow worms illuminating the forest floor. At first Tapapriya held onto Laxmi's hand so tightly her fingers hurt. Every small sound made her jump. But soon she became mesmerized by the twinkling lights below and reflected in the spiderwebs above. She forgot about her fear as they tried to catch the sparkling insects in jars.

When it was finally time to head home, complete darkness had fallen. Tapapriya froze in panic. "I can't see anything! What if we lose our way?" she cried.

Laxmi rummaged in her pocket and pulled out a small piece of limestone she had collected earlier. "We can use this to light the way," she said, striking it against a flint stone. A spark ignited and a tiny flame appeared, just enough to illuminate the path directly in front of them.

Tapapriya was amazed. "You mean fire can help us not be afraid?"

Laxmi nodded. "That's right. As long as we have a little light, we'll be okay."

From that day on, Tapapriya began to overcome her fear bit by bit. She started staying out later in the forest and using leaves or sticks to make small lamps. She discovered fire not only keeps scary creatures away, but also reveals new nocturnal wonders like owls, bats and night-blooming flowers.

One night, there was no moon and the forest was exceptionally dark. Tapapriya and Laxmi had wandered deeper than ever before, playing a game of hide and seek. But when it was time to seek each other, Tapapriya realized she had become lost. Panic rose in her chest until she remembered her lamp. Lighting a twig, she saw footprints in the dirt and followed them until she found Laxmi waiting for her, relieved but proud.

"You did it Tapapriya!" Laxmi said. "You faced the dark all by yourself."

From that moment on, Tapapriya was no longer afraid of the night. She had overcome her fear with the help of her clever friend and the gift of fire's warm glow. The forest held no more unseen dangers - only adventure to discover through the darkness.

Tiny Droplet

I was just a tiny droplet floating high up in the fluffy white clouds, feeling bored. All the other raindrops were playing around me, swimming in little pools formed on the bottom of the clouds. But I wanted an adventure! I looked down longingly at the green fields and forests stretching as far as I could see below the clouds.

"I wish I could get down there and explore," I thought. Just then, a strong gust of wind blew through the clouds, shaking them up. I felt myself lift up and get swept away in the wind current. "Whoooa!" I cried out as I tumbled head over heels, spinning wildly. The other raindrops called out "Good luck!" as I got blown away from the safety of the clouds.

My heart pounded with excitement as I got carried further and further down by the gusts. The clouds drew nearer as I passed through them, hitting millions of tiny water droplets. I could see the ground approaching rapidly below. As I emerged from the last cloud, the strong sunlight hit me. "Aaah it's so bright down here!" I yelled, trying to shield my eyes with my tiny arms.

Whoosh! A giant leaf swooped down and caught me as I fell. I clung onto it for dear life as the wind tossed it around. It was a wild ride! As the leaf did flip flops and somersaults in the air, I saw the beautiful landscapes spread out below - fields of golden wheat swaying in the breeze, colorful wildflowers dotting the meadows and rolling green hills in the distance.

"Wow what a view!" I exclaimed in wonder. But just then, the leaf hit an air current that slammed it hard onto the ground. "Ooof!" I cried as I lost my grip and rolled off. The impact shook me but I wasn't hurt. I looked up to see the leaf had landed right beside a little red flower. Its petals were drooping sadly, missing the sunlight now blocked by the huge leaf above it.

"Don't worry little flower, I'll help you," I said. I gathered all my strength and began pushing against the leaf with all my might. It was so heavy but I didn't give up. After much pushing and shoving, the leaf finally budged an inch. Encouraged, I pushed even harder and slowly, it started to move further. The flower perked up, its petals standing up straighter as more sunlight fell on it.

By the time I rolled out, exhausted, from under the leaf, the flower was glowing brightly, fully facing the sun once again. "Thank you, raindrop friend! You saved me," it said gratefully. I beamed with pride. Just then, dark clouds started rolling in above us, rumbling ominously. "Looks like rain is coming. You should find shelter!" the flower advised.

I bid it goodbye and rolled away quickly across the field, looking for cover. The clouds opened up then, letting loose a downpour. The fat raindrops fell all around me as I sped for shelter, dodging between the blades of grass. Ahead, I spotted a hollow tree stump and dived inside just in time! Curling up against the damp wood, I watched the heavy rain fall in sheets outside.

Suddenly, the sky brightened and the rain stopped as quickly as it had started. Cautiously peeking out, I gasped at the beautiful sight that greeted me - the whole meadow glistened with millions of raindrops, glittering and glowing like crystals in the afternoon sun. A colorful rainbow arched across the sky in the distance. It was the most amazing sight ever.

I had the best adventure a lone raindrop could ask for - floating in clouds, sailing on leaves, meeting new friends and hurrying through fields and flowers. Now as evening drew near, it was time to return home. I rolled back to the edge of the meadow and looked up longingly at the cottony white clouds floating by in the orange sky. A gust of wind lifted me up and back into the waiting clouds where I belonged. Soon, I drifted off to sleep, dreaming of my rainy-day adventure and the wonderful sights I had seen below.

About the Author

Sayan Panda

The author of this delightful children's short story book is Sayan Panda, a talented writer with a passion for storytelling. Sayan has an impressive literary background, having written 11 books prior to this one. His previous works spanned various genres, including thrillers, horror, and satirical stories, showcasing his versatility as a writer.

Outside of his writing pursuits, Sayan is also a dedicated school teacher, bringing his creativity and love for storytelling into the classroom. His passion for education and his understanding of children's interests and imaginations shines through in his captivating stories.

In this enchanting children's short story book, Sayan Panda weaves together magical tales that will transport young readers to fascinating worlds filled with adventure, friendship, and valuable life lessons. With his skillful storytelling and vivid imagination, Sayan has created a collection of stories that will capture the hearts and minds of children, sparking their imagination and encouraging a love for reading.

www.ingramcontent.com/pod-product-compliance
Lightning Source LLC
LaVergne TN
LVHW041539070526
838199LV00046B/1748